MAX'S MAGICAL
DREAM

MAX'S MAGICAL DREAM

Gillian Overitt

Book Guild Publishing
Sussex, England

First published in Great Britain in 2012 by
The Book Guild Ltd
Pavilion View
19 New Road
Brighton, BN1 1UF

Typesetting in Century Schoolbook and Helvetica by
Keyboard Services, Luton, Bedfordshire

Printed in Great Britain by
CPI Group (UK) Ltd, Croydon, CR0 4YY

A catalogue record for this book is available from
The British Library.

ISBN 978 1 84624 718 7

1

The Painting

Max stood and stretched his arms up above his head. He had spent a long time going through his comics and he now had two piles in front of him on the floor; one for keeping, the other for throwing away. That would please his mum as she had been nagging him to sort through them all week. There were only two comics in the 'pile for throwing away' but he still felt proud of himself. Parting with any of his precious comics was always very difficult. He picked them up and threw them across the room into the bin. He frowned as the bin – on being hit sideways by the comics – fell over. Sweet wrappers, rubber bands and a crisp packet fell out onto the floor. He was going to pick them up when suddenly something caught his eye. It was the loft ladder.

Max's dad had been up in the loft looking for something earlier. Max knew that his father had completely forgotten to put the ladder away and had wandered off to do something else. In Max's imagination, the ladder transformed into a steep mountain disappearing into dark clouds above...

Max put on his hiking boots and checked that he had his coat zipped up to his chin. He set off to climb the mountain. It was steeper than he had realised and he had to use all his strength to haul himself up the mountainside. He stopped halfway up to pull out his water bottle. He took a long drink while holding tightly onto a jagged piece of rock. He put the bottle back into the side of his rucksack and started the journey again. His foot slipped and he just managed to cling onto the rock face as large stones rolled down into the abyss. Eventually he reached the top of the mountain and pulled himself safely onto the plateau...

Max peered around him as he tried to make out the different shapes in the gloom of the loft. He knew he wasn't supposed to be there, but he wasn't going to let a prick of conscience put him off. Just across from the hatch was something that was just catching the light. Max was drawn like a moth to a flame; he went over and picked up what appeared to be a picture in a mirrored frame. He stepped back so that he could see it more clearly.

He couldn't help but say 'Wow!' and immediately wished he had not. He listened, but with some relief realised that his parents hadn't heard him. He wiped the dust off the picture with the sleeve of his jumper and stared at it as he held it out in front of him. There stood a bright green dragon, with yellow eyes and fire in the colours of vermilion and daffodil yellow curling out from its mouth. Smoke came out in puffs from its large nostrils. Its tail seemed to go on forever into the distance. The dragon took up almost the entire picture, but just in the right-hand corner could be seen a little castle. Max strained to see it clearly in the darkness of the loft. He was sure there was a figure looking out of one of the towers of the castle, but it was much too small to see properly.

Max decided he must take the picture down to his bedroom to get a better look at it. He carefully lowered himself down the ladder, holding on tightly to this fascinating treasure. He reached his bedroom safely and propped it up against his bed. The picture was in fact a painting; Max thought it must be quite new as the colours were so bright. He examined the figure but could still not see it clearly. Then Max remembered the present his Uncle John had given him last Christmas. He opened the bottom drawer of his bedside cupboard and pulled out a shiny new magnifying glass which he placed over the picture and to his satisfaction, everything became clear. The figure was that of a girl, a little younger than himself, leaning out of the window of the tower. She had reddish-coloured hair that flowed down to her elbows and was wearing a pink dress with lace around the neck and cuffs.

Max was about to put the glass away when he caught sight of something else on the painting; a figure riding a big white horse. He thought it very strange that he hadn't noticed it before. He looked more closely, but it was impossible to see very much. The only thing he could make out was that the figure was dressed in shining armour. Just then, he heard the sound of footsteps upon the stairs and quickly pushed the painting under his bed, picking up one of his comics to pretend he was reading. His dad put his head around the bedroom door and seeing Max apparently engrossed in his comic, he smiled and went to put the loft ladder away.

That night as Max went to bed, he pulled the painting out to have one last look. His attention was drawn to the figure on the horse and he was puzzled by why he hadn't noticed it at first. He also wondered whose painting it was, as it was not the sort of thing his mum would have liked and he very much doubted it was his dad's. At the age of nine it is really difficult to imagine your dad – who is interested in cars and football – ever being interested in dragons. Max put the painting back into its hiding place and got into bed. Unusually for him, he felt really tired and went straight to sleep...

Maximilliun was feeling hot and tired. His suit of armour was heavy and it was digging into his neck. His handsome steed, Silver, was still full of energy. Silver was a beautiful horse with strong legs and a shiny mane that shimmered as he galloped. After having gone over land and lakes and mountains, Maximilliun was at last nearing the valley of Dakas the Dragon. The sun was just setting and he could see the silhouette of the castle, but there seemed to be no sign of the dragon. Maximilliun was not sure whether this was a good thing. Was it better to see your enemy or not? For surely if you could see them, they could also see you?

Then suddenly, as if his thoughts had been heard, a long spine-chilling roar pierced the silence. Silver reared up, startled by the noise. Maximilliun just about managed to hold on to the reins and cling to the sides of his horse with his legs. As Silver's front hoofs hit the ground, Maximilliun felt a fearful shiver go through his body. Coming out of the shadows, far closer than Max would have liked, stood Dakas. The dragon's eyes were a fluorescent yellow that seemed to light up the whole area. Where the dragon had been hiding Maximilliun could only guess; its body was green all over and was perfectly camouflaged to blend into the surrounding area.

Maximilliun was trying to work out what to do next, while at the same time speaking gently to try to calm Silver. His efforts came abruptly to an end as Dakas the Dragon stretched to his full height, opened his jaws wide and ejected a powerful burst of flames in their direction. It was only because Maximilliun had expected this that they managed to back off before the flames could reach them. Dakas watched Maximilliun and his horse as they fled for cover behind a rock. Smoke came out of the dragon's nostrils and his eyes glared into the quickening darkness. The sun was almost set.

Maximilliun jumped down from Silver and stroked his neck with affection. Silver turned his head and nudged his master in response. 'I'm going to have to go on without you, Silver,' said Maximilliun. 'I don't think it will be safe to take you any closer to that monster and it's possible I can sneak by unseen on my own! Go back to the edge of the woods and wait there for me.' Silver nodded slightly to tell his master that he understood. Maximilliun watched as Silver slowly trotted off and he suddenly felt very alone.

Sometime later, when Maximilliun had taken some of his armour off, he set off to do the job he had come to do. Whether or not he would be able to rescue the girl in the castle he didn't know. He did know that ahead of him was one of the most dangerous dragons that had ever been seen and he was not sure how he would defeat him. He must move quietly and try and stop his knees from shaking.

In the morning when Max pulled out the painting, he was very surprised to see that the rider and horse had gone. In their place stood a large rock.

2

Maximilliun and the Dragon

Max found it difficult to concentrate at school that day. His dream the night before had seemed so real. As for the painting, that was indeed very strange. Maybe he had just imagined that the horse and rider had been in the painting. Maybe when he looked at it in the morning, because he had been dreaming, he had imagined the rock being there. It was all too confusing! Then there was the problem with Mum. When she had come in to see if he was getting up, she said she smelt smoke. Smoke! What was all that about? She even accused him of playing with matches in the bedroom. As if he would!

Max had been told off for daydreaming several times that morning and even he decided it had to stop. He made a big effort to try to concentrate on his spelling in the afternoon but he still found his mind wandering. At the end of the lessons, Mrs Pike had said she hoped he would apply himself better tomorrow, whatever that meant. He went home half hoping that the painting had just disappeared. His friend Tom wanted to know why he was being so quiet, but Max was sure he would think he had gone crazy if he told him. So he didn't. He managed to change the subject and he even forgot about his troubles on the way home. However, as soon as he walked through the back door, even before Mum called 'Hi!', it all came back to him.

'Hello, Sunshine, what sort of day have you had? Did you have a spelling test?' asked Mum as she went to meet him in the kitchen.

'I wish you wouldn't call me that. What if Tom had come back with me?' replied Max grumpily.

'Oh, we're in a bit of a mood are we?' Mum said as she ruffled his hair. Max pulled away crossly. He wished she wouldn't treat him like a baby.

'I'm just tired, that's all.'

'You must be sickening for something, you don't usually admit to being tired. You did go to sleep quickly last night, I noticed. Are you all right, Max?' Mum spoke kindly and Max felt mean for being cross with her.

'I'll be fine, Mum,' he said. 'Maybe I just need a glass of milk and a chocolate biscuit. I'm sure I'll be all right then.' Max really wanted to dash off up to his bedroom and pull out the painting, but he knew that he would only arouse her suspicion.

'I'm sure you're right Max,' said Mum, smiling as she went to get the biscuit tin. Max took them from her and helped himself to a big chocolate one. He waited while his mum poured out a glass of milk and handed it to him. At last he had the opportunity to go and look at the painting again.

'Don't go spilling the milk all the way up the stairs,' called Mum. As Max made his way up to his bedroom he found it a struggle to go slowly. He knew that his mum was still watching him and he desperately wanted to get upstairs without any more delays.

Having put down his milk and biscuit on his dressing table, he knelt down on the floor in front of his bed. Part of him wanted to pull the painting out quickly but the other part of him was afraid to. 'Get on with it!' he told himself, then leant forward and quickly pulled the painting out. There was the dragon, looking so fierce and powerful; beside it stood the rock. In the corner of the painting was the castle. The figure still stood there just as it had done before. He got out his magnifying glass and searched the painting. There was no sign of the mounted rider, no sign at all.

It was some time later – when he had eaten the biscuit and drunk the milk – that Max came to a decision. It was simple; he had imagined the rider after having had the dream. He was not going mad; it was all just his imagination. He pushed the painting away and went downstairs to watch some TV.

When he went to bed that night, Max didn't think much about the dragon and didn't bother to pull out the painting for another look. He decided that he would wait until the loft was open again and put it back – it had caused him enough trouble. So he climbed into bed and read for a little while. Dad came in to say goodnight, which Max certainly hoped it would be! He certainly didn't want another night filled with strange dreams.

Maximilliun crept out from behind the rock. He crouched low behind some trees and listened carefully for any signs of the dragon. His heart seemed to be so loud that he wondered if the dragon could hear it. Even his breathing sounded to him like a badly-tuned violin in a library. Maximilliun wanted to go back to Silver and ride away; ride a long way away from the dragon. His legs didn't take any notice of his thoughts and continued to carry him on towards the castle.

Suddenly a light shone from high above. He looked up and just caught a shadow passing by a window in the tower furthest from him, then froze as a familiar sound broke the silence of the night. It was Dakas, roaring again but this time facing away from him. Maybe the dragon was warning the girl that he was still there, guarding the castle, keeping her trapped. This thought made Maximilliun more determined to conquer his fear and continue on towards his goal. He made a quick dash while the dragon was busy showing off his fiery fury. He just managed to get to a tree that was close to the castle wall when Dakas settled back down. Again, the dragon seemed to disappear into the vegetation. Maximilliun shook his head in astonishment.

Maximilliun stood by the tree for some time. There was nothing to hide him from view if he left the tree and he couldn't think how he could get by the dragon without being seen. The minutes ticked by but no brilliant idea came. If he held back until the dragon got up for another display of his fiery power, he may have a very long wait. He sat down quietly as he could think of nothing else to do. He made himself as comfortable as he could. It had been a long journey and now night had come. Maximilliun struggled to stay awake, but his aching tired body won the battle and he drifted off into a deep sleep.

Maximilliun woke with a start. There was an awful sound from behind him. Dakas had found his hiding place and flames were shooting from his mouth. Maximilliun looked in horror as the tree that had been shielding him began to burn, then a flame caught his trouser leg and he rolled over on the grass to put it out. He realised that the noise had stopped and looking up, he found himself gazing straight into Dakas' yellow eyes. They looked as though they alone were enough to burn through him. Then Dakas opened his jaws and as Maximilliun started to run, there was a deep throaty roar and he knew that the fire would be next.

Max was holding his ears with his hands to cut out the noise.

'Max... I won't tell you again. Get up! You're going to make us all late,' shouted Mum as she pulled back the duvet. 'And there is no point in you holding your ears, you still have to get up,' she said as she saw her son curled up with his eyes tight shut. Max opened his eyes and was so relieved that once again, he had just been dreaming. In fact he was so happy, he surprised his mum by jumping out of bed and giving her a hug.

'And you won't get round me like that!' said Mum, trying not to smile. 'You know, I can still smell smoke in here. I think I'll close your window today ... it must be coming in from outside.' His mum closed the window and went downstairs.

Max rushed around getting ready for school. As he did so, he remembered that it was Friday. He liked Fridays because they did sports in the morning

11

and painting in the afternoon. He also liked it because it meant that tomorrow was Saturday and Dad had promised to take him down to see the football match in the town. West Hampstead were going to play Brocklehurst at home; it was sure to be such a great game! They were taking Tom too, so they would have a lot to talk about today. He was just thinking about whether his favourite striker Geoff Martin would be playing, when something caught his attention. He stood with his mouth open as he looked down at his pyjama bottoms. They were singed on the right leg, all the way up to his knee. Max slumped to his knees as he realised what this meant. Somehow when he went to sleep he became Maximilliun; this was a real life adventure! He knew that he had to keep this a secret and quickly took off his pyjama bottoms so that he could hide them under some old toys in his wardrobe. Then he pulled out the painting, knowing it would be different even before he saw it – and it was. The dragon was standing side-on this time, obscuring most of the castle. There was the girl at the window looking out and at the edge, a burnt tree. Beside the tree was a figure. Max didn't need to get out his magnifying glass to know that the figure was desperately trying to get away from the dragon, or that the face of the figure was a picture of great fear; he already knew.

The day seemed to pass very quickly. Max could not understand how the good days went so fast, while the days he did not like seemed to go on forever. He suspected that that would be one of the things he had yet to learn.

Max was allowed to stay up an hour later on Fridays, so that night he went to bed feeling really sleepy. He refused to think about Maximilliun and the dragon; instead he thought about the match and was sure that Geoff Martin would get at least two goals. He hoped that they would get good seats and be able to see the whole match easily. Then he started to imagine playing alongside Geoff and passing him the winning goal.

There was a smile on Max's face as he drifted off to sleep.

3

Inside the Castle

Maximilliun could feel the heat all the way down his back as he ran as fast as he could. He was glad he had taken off the bottom half of his armour, as he would have stood no chance at all with its weight slowing him down. It was so dark, he had no idea where he was going. Suddenly he was running downhill. Then there was a large splash as Maximilliun fell face-down into a river. Fortunately, it wasn't very deep or it would have drowned him in no time at all; there was no way he would have been able to swim with his helmet and upper body armour on. He looked around for Dakas, who was hiding behind a large puff of smoke nearby. Having made such a splash in the water, Maximilliun must have put the dragon's fire out!

Dakas was very annoyed at losing his power. He knew from experience that it would take some time to get his flame back and so he decided to go back into his garden to wait. He was sure that his enemy would have been well and truly frightened off. Many others had tried but he always won. Usually just one show of his mighty strength and that was enough to scare off even the bravest knight. Those that were sensible knew it would be hopeless to try and meddle any more with the Great Dakas. So the large beast settled down

14

for a sleep, quite content that his job was done. However, Dakas had never met such a determined person as Maximilliun before. If he had, he would not have drifted off so easily.

Maximilliun was relieved to hear the sound of the dragon walking away from him. Carefully, he got out of the water and climbed the steep bank. He left a trail of water behind him, not to mention a couple of very surprised frogs. When he reached the top of the bank, he followed the line of the river until he was sure he had put enough distance between himself and Dakas. Then he took off his armour and the rest of his clothes. He squeezed his trousers and shirt until he had got most of the water out and was surprised to see how burnt his trousers were, but pleased his leg was unharmed! He decided he would leave his armour behind, as he felt sure it would be easier to get past the dragon more quietly without it. He put the rest of his clothes on; they clung to his body as they were still very damp. Maximilliun hid his armour beneath a nearby bush and started out once more for the castle.

Several minutes later, Maximilliun was right up beside the side wall of the castle. The moon had come out and was shining down so that he could just about see where he was. There was no entrance along this wall and he knew the only way in was to go around to the front of the castle. Carefully, he felt his way along the side of the wall. He could hear the sound of breathing and the occasional snore. He knew that Dakas was not far away. A shiver went down his spine; he knew that once he reached the front of the castle, he would be very close to the dragon – too close for comfort. A sensible person would go back, he thought. Then he remembered that he was not known for being sensible and furthermore 'being sensible' was not going to save the girl in the tower!

He took a few more steps, when suddenly he felt himself falling. Down and down he fell, eventually coming to land on a pile of sacks. They were full of something hard and Maximilliun knew he was going to be bruised all over. Fortunately, it all happened so quickly that he didn't have time to cry out. He stood up and strained his eyes to see where he was. The light of the moon shone down on him and he could just make out his surroundings. He was in the castle at last and it was as much as he could do to stop himself from shouting out in joy. His next task was to find the tower!

Maximilliun climbed off the sacks and moved forward slowly until he felt the cold hard stone that was the wall of the cellar. He moved sideways with his hands touching the wall as he went. A couple of times he nearly fell over things that were on the floor. He knew that eventually he would come to a door. He reached a corner and continued on until he came across the sacks that he had landed upon earlier. At least he could now see a little better and so he continued to work his way round the sacks until he found the wall again. He was just moving sideways when a tremor seemed to pass through the castle. There was a pause, and then it happened again. Maximilliun was afraid that the dragon had found out where he was and was making his way to him. He stood still, feeling the tremors that were now accompanied with a noise. He was sure it had to be the dragon, and suddenly felt very tired, cold and scared.

Meanwhile, Dakas had woken up from the short sleep and was feeling very hungry. He knew his power was still not back properly; what he needed was a good feast. The dragon pulled himself up from his resting place and went round to the side of the castle to where he was usually fed. The dragon looked around and sniffed the air, but was quite sure that he could not detect any signs of the intruder. Once at the feeding spot, he let out a very loud growl. To Maximilliun, it sounded like a clap of thunder and it made him shrink against the cold wall. Dakas, unaware of the fear he was creating just a few feet below, growled again. Then, as if that wasn't enough, he jumped up and down a couple of times. Maximilliun thought the walls would fall down. Then everything went eerily quiet. Maximilliun didn't dare to breathe and it was all he could do to stop his teeth from chattering.

After a few seconds, although it felt like forever to Maximilliun, there came a noise from within the castle. It sounded like chains rattling, combined with a strange squeaking sound. Then a door opened to his right. Light streamed through the door giving a silhouette to a tall, stout figure. The figure was pushing a trolley that had two large buckets on it. Maximilliun remained as still as a statue. The figure spoke to the dragon in an unusual accent.

'You're up early, Dakas!' he said. 'You eat too much and you'll be getting fat. Then what good would you be? What use is a fat dragon, eh?' Dakas responded with another growl. Maximilliun took the opportunity to dash from his hiding place, through the door and off along a corridor. The escape had not gone unnoticed. When Maximilliun reached a flight of stairs, he looked back and saw the man's face clearly. It was for just a split second, but he saw the look of surprise. He noticed that the man had shoulder-length hair the colour of snow. He also had a short beard and must have been at least a hundred years old, as he had lots of wrinkles. As Maximilliun climbed the stairs two at a time, he wondered why this old man was looking after the dragon. Perhaps he was the one that had originally captured the girl? It looked like he had more than one enemy to get past; but first he needed to find the prisoner.

When he reached the top of the stairs, he had two options. He could go left, along a dark corridor or right, along a dark corridor. He chose to go left. He ran as quickly as he dared into the darkness. He was sure that the man would be coming after him. His only consolation was that the man was not only old but also quite fat, and wouldn't be able to move quickly. However, Maximilliun was totally unaware of the other dangers within the castle walls. A short distance ahead sat a very large spider. It was not just large but enormous. It filled the whole of the corridor and its legs were splayed out into two rooms on either side. Maximilliun continued to run straight into it. The spider immediately wrapped him round and round with its silky strings. Maximilliun, being unable to see very clearly, had no idea what had scooped him off his feet and tied him so expertly and so quickly.

Maximiliun could feel himself being lifted and carried away. The spider was making its way to its web, high in a corner of the castle's main entrance hall. Suddenly, a girl jumped out in front of them and shouted for the spider to stop.

'Where do you think you are taking that boy?' she asked with her hands on her hips. 'Put him down. You cannot eat him. He will be much too chewy and probably make you quite sick.'

The spider did not reply, as this spider had never learnt to talk. It did understand the girl and dropped its parcel on the floor in front of her. Maximilliun wasn't hurt when he was dropped, because the spider's silk was so thick. He hit the floor and rolled over and over. Finally, he came to a standstill by the girl's feet. Whilst he had been rolling, some of the spider's web had unravelled. Once he had come to a complete

18

stop, he pulled the remaining strands from his face. First, he saw the girl and then looked up into the face of the monster spider. His face changed to the colour of his mum's white sheets on washing day and although he wanted to speak, he found he could not. Instead, he fainted.

It was some time later that Maximilliun woke up. He thought at first that he was dreaming, for there was a girl leaning over him. He thought that she looked like an angel. She had very blonde hair that reached down to her waist. It was very curly and shone as it caught the light of the candle she was holding. She had a creamy-coloured dress on with a crisp, white apron on top. The girl's eyes were brown and very big. She smiled down at Maximilliun, and it was several seconds before she spoke.

'I'm glad you have awakened,' she said. Maximilliun thought her voice was beautiful, as it sounded like the wind whistling through the trees. He couldn't think of anything to say to this and so he said nothing.

'You need not worry about Crawler; he is perfectly well-behaved when I am around.'

Maximilliun suddenly remembered the giant spider and felt faint again. This time though, he was determined to control himself. It was bad enough that he had fainted the first time in front of this angel; he certainly was not going to do it again.

'Crawler?' he asked, trying desperately to keep his voice steady.

'Yes, Crawler. He's my pet spider. And before you say it, I know it's slightly strange to have a spider for a pet. And I also know that he is a little big.'

'A little big – you can say that again!' Maximilliun looked around the room expecting to see the monster spider, but he could not.

19

'I know, but he needs someone to look after him. I was just sitting there one day and along he came.'

'Didn't he frighten you?'

'Of course he did at first, but you know, he didn't mean to. Crawler was just being friendly.'

Maximilliun suddenly realised that he was still lying on the floor with several strands of silk wrapped around him. He pulled them off and got up. When he stood up, he was surprised that the girl was quite small and she looked even more angelic. As she smiled, it seemed as though she were laughing at him.

'What? What's up?' Maximilliun asked.

'I was just wondering what a brave young man like you was doing here,' she replied, her smile still twinkling in her eyes.

Maximilliun liked being called 'a brave young man' and stretched himself up to make himself look even more impressive. 'I'm here to rescue the girl from the tower,' he said, proudly.

The girl laughed and then suddenly put her hand over her mouth in an attempt to quieten her mirth. 'I'm sure you'll do that very well; yes, very well indeed!' Then she turned around and flew away. At least, that's how it seemed to Maximilliun. He didn't hear her footsteps. The last thing he saw going through the doorway was a vision of floating cream material that was the train of her dress. He stood for a while looking after her, unable to move and not wanting to anyway.

Max got out of bed feeling very excited. There was a couple of seconds before he remembered why he was excited. Then a smile spread over his face. Of course, he thought, today was the day of the match!

He was just going to rush downstairs when a shadow came across his thoughts. The dream came back to him and he shivered with the thought of that awful spider. He pulled the painting out from its hiding place under his bed. The dragon had gone and the picture was completely different. The castle stood where the dragon had done before. There were several floors with many windows. Right at the top of one tower stood the girl in pink. Four flights below, there was the girl with the cream dress, sitting in candlelight. A flight below that was the boy looking out and just one window away could be seen a shadow. Max got out his magnifying glass and pulled the painting nearer to the window; he felt his heart race as he saw that the figure was that of the man that had been in the cellar. This figure was just a room away from Maximilliun who was motionless. Max knew that he would not want to go to bed that night. He didn't want to know what would happen next...

4

Max Talks to Tom

Max found that his original excitement about the day had gone. He tried hard to stop thinking about the latest picture on the painting, but he couldn't. He went downstairs to find his mum taking washing out of the machine. She turned in surprise at seeing Max.

'You're an early bird!' she said as Max stood in the doorway, looking as though he didn't know why he was there.

'It's the match today; Tom's coming round soon,' he replied, trying to smile but failing badly.

'Well, you don't seem too happy about it. Is there something wrong?'

'No... I'm fine. I didn't sleep too well, that's all. I'm starving. Have we got any Coco Pops?' Max went over to the cupboard and got out a bowl. He opened the cupboard where the cereal was kept, but he couldn't see his favourite. 'Oh Mum, you didn't get any!' he said accusingly.

'I did, so stop complaining. They're behind the Cornflakes. My, you are a grumpy thing aren't you?'

Max found the cereal and settled down to his breakfast. Just as he was tucking into his second mouthful, his mother closed the door of the washing machine and picked up one of Max's pyjama tops. 'Max, you don't know where your pyjama bottoms are, do you?' she asked.

'Er ... no. I thought I put them in the wash with the top,' he said, trying not to drop Coco Pops from his mouth.

'They don't seem to be here. That's strange; I'll have another look later. Perhaps they got tangled up with something else.' She went into the garden to hang the wet clothes out to dry.

Max ate his breakfast without really enjoying it. He didn't like lying to his mum and was feeling really guilty. There was no way he could have told her the truth, he told himself. She would never believe him. She would say he had been playing with the matches. Max was sure that if he showed her the painting it would break the magic and although he was frightened about what was going to happen next in the dream, he had no choice but to find out. Once he had finished his breakfast, he dashed upstairs to his bedroom, found an old carrier bag in the bottom of his wardrobe and grabbed his burnt pyjama trousers from beneath the toys. As he pushed them into the bag, he noticed that they were wet as well as singed. He tied up the top of the bag quickly and put it into the backpack he would be taking to the match.

Tom arrived at one o'clock, in plenty of time, as they did not need to leave for the match until quarter past two. Max had decided what to do and felt a lot happier. He would tell his friend all about the painting and the dreams. He didn't really know why he hadn't told him before; he had shared everything with Tom since they had met on their first day of school. That was over five years now and Max knew that they would always be friends, and friends – good friends – always shared secrets. So when Tom arrived, Max rushed him upstairs to his bedroom and closed the door.

'Tom, I've got something really important to tell you!' he started. Tom took his bag from his shoulder and threw it onto the bed. He looked at his friend and knew instantly that it was something exciting. Max did this funny thing with his eyes when he was excited. He raised his eyebrows high and his eyes seemed to jump out of their sockets.

'I knew there was something!' he replied as he bounced onto Max's bed.

'Now, this is a big secret and you have to promise not to tell anyone.' Max was talking quite quietly now for he did not want to be overheard. Tom nodded and gave Max his full attention.

'It all started when I got this painting from the loft the other day. It was of a castle and a large dragon. In one of the towers there was a figure and there was also a horse and rider in the background...'

'So where is this painting now?' asked Tom. Max pulled the painting out from under his bed. Tom jumped down to get a closer look.

'But where's the dragon? I can't see it. It is just a picture of a castle.'

'That's the whole point! Look, when I go to sleep at night, I dream about the painting and in the morning the picture has changed.' He looked at Tom as if he should now understand perfectly.

'I'm sorry Max, but you're losing me. How can a painting change? And what do you mean, you have dreams?'

It took Max another ten minutes to explain fully to Tom what had been happening. Tom still looked as though he didn't quite believe what he was hearing, so Max took out the carrier bag from his backpack. He undid the knot and dropped the pyjama trousers out onto the floor. Tom stared at the pyjamas with his mouth open in wonder.

'Max, they're burnt and wet!' he said as he picked up the trousers at arm's length with one finger and thumb. Max let his friend ponder on this thought. Then Tom dropped the trousers and looked up at Max's smiling face. Tom smiled back.

'Wow, this is a real adventure!' he said, almost in a whisper.

'It is, but we have to keep it between ourselves or I'm sure it will all disappear. I have to know what happens! But there's something we have to do. We have to get rid of these pyjamas. If Mum finds them, I'll be grounded for the whole of the summer.' He started to push the pyjama bottoms back into the bag and tie it up again.

'I thought we could take them to the match and "lose" them in one of the bins there,' he continued as he put the bundle into his backpack.

'That's the best idea. I mean, if you put them into

your own bin, your mum or dad might find them and then how on earth could you explain it?' Tom was pushing his fingers through his fair hair and leaving it sticking out at all angles. 'Well, I just wish I could be in your dreams. I would be a knight on a jet-black horse. I would fly across the river and straight up to the dragon. Then I would gallop away and distract the dragon so that Maximilliun could rescue the fair maiden.' Tom started to gallop around the room as if he were on a horse.

'That's very brave of you, I'm sure, but what about the man with the white hair?' replied Max as he grabbed Tom to stop him jumping about.

'Yes, well, as soon as I had led the dragon into a big pit, I would gallop back and storm the castle gates. I would shout and blow a horn to distract the man. So while I'm busy, Maximilliun would be able to dash off to rescue the damsel in distress.' Tom began to blow his imaginary horn.

'That's if the giant spider doesn't get you first, you mean.'

'Oh dear, I forgot about that. I hate spiders. There was one in the bathroom last night and I didn't hang around, I can tell you.' Tom pulled a funny face as he remembered the spider.

'You wouldn't like this one, then. It was at least as big as a bus.'

'Don't you worry, I would have the largest sharpest sword and I would dig it straight into its heart.' Tom demonstrated with his imaginary sword and then wiped it with his fingers to get the blood off.

'Ouch!' he said, hopping about. 'I've cut myself now.'

Max started to laugh and that set Tom off, too. They just about heard a voice from downstairs shouting 'Are you two coming, or am I going to the match on my own?' It was Dad. Both boys shouted back 'Coming!', grabbed their bags and still laughing, went down to meet him.

Max managed to dispose of the pyjama bottoms quite easily on a trip to the toilets. Getting rid of them felt like a load had been taken from him and he felt much happier. The match was great. By half time, there had been no score but just ten minutes from the end of the match, Geoff Martin had steamed past the goalie with a real winner. The stadium was in uproar as West Hampstead fans shouted out their excitement. The remainder of the match was quite tense and Max was glad when the final whistle blew. Both boys jumped up and down, as Dad looked on with a broad smile on his face.

The journey home was full of talk about the match. Tom was dropped off first and Dad took Max to the fish and chip shop to get their supper.

That night, as Max lay in his bed, he sighed; it had been a very exciting day. There was no place in his thoughts for the painting. Max slept contentedly.

5

Max and Tom Meet the New Girl

Max stretched himself out in his bed and the quilt fell onto the floor. He got out of bed, put on his slippers and raced downstairs. He just arrived in the kitchen when he suddenly remembered something.

'I didn't dream!' he said out loud.

'What's that, Sunshine?' called Mum from the lounge.

'Oh, nothing Mum,' replied Max. The fact that he had not had a dream made him feel really disappointed. Then he remembered what the painting looked like and thought that maybe it was a good thing. He started to get himself a bowl of cereal while Mum made them both a cup of hot chocolate.

After breakfast, Max went upstairs and pulled out the painting. He stared at it for some time but he was sure that it was just the same as it had been the day before. He reluctantly pushed it back under the bed. Maybe, he thought, that would be the end of these strange dreams. Perhaps sharing the secret with Tom had been a mistake after all. He felt sad to think that he wouldn't know whether the girl got rescued from the tower. He pulled out the painting again, but it looked just the same as before. Sadly, he pushed it back under his bed.

That night, as Max dressed for bed, he remembered the dreams and sighed. In truth, he had been finding it difficult to think about anything else all day. The day had been the sort that he usually loved; cycling with Dad in the morning, a roast dinner with chocolate pudding and ice cream for dessert and the rest of the day going through his comics. Somehow he found it difficult to really enjoy any of it. At the back of his mind had been the worry that he would never again dream about the castle and have the chance to be a hero. Max was in bed for ages tossing and turning; he wanted to go to sleep but was afraid to. Eventually, tiredness won the battle and he slept soundly.

It was barely light when Max woke up. He jumped out of bed and pulled the painting out, blinking his eyes in an effort to see but it was too dark. He got up and pulled back the curtains. Light streamed into the room and fell across the painting. Max looked at it; nothing had changed but he was not really surprised. As he had not dreamt, he was not really expecting it to be different. He climbed back into his bed and went to sleep.

Tom noticed that there was something wrong with his friend as soon as he saw him. Max arrived for school just as the whistle went and Tom had no chance to speak to him until they reached the cloakroom.

'What's up Max?' he asked. You don't look very happy today...'

'I haven't had any more dreams. I think telling you about them must have been the wrong thing to do,' replied Max as he hung up his coat.

'Oh Max, I'm sorry.'

'It's not your fault. How could you know? I mean, how would I have known that's what would happen? Am I making any sense?'

'I'm not sure ... but I think I know what you are trying to say.' Then Mrs Pike came out of the classroom and Max and Tom had to delay their discussion until playtime.

Later on, Max and Tom discussed the problem some more but couldn't solve the mystery. Tom tried to cheer his friend up but found his impersonations of Mr Clarkson, the teacher of year four, failed to move Max into laughter as it usually did. They both went back into class feeling sad.

At lunchtime, Tom tried to make his friend laugh again but Max wasn't in the right mood. In the end, Tom decided to talk to Max about the dreams.

'I think it's really sad that your dreams have come to an end. They were a real adventure, weren't they?' he started.

'They were fun. I suppose that's what I'm most upset about. It was good to have the dream and then wake up to find the painting had changed.'

'Well, we can carry on the story if you like. You can be Maximilliun. How do you know that's what his name was, anyway?'

'I suppose I just sort of made it up. I mean you don't have any control over your dreams, do you?'

'No, I suppose not, dreams really are strange aren't they? Anyway you can be Maximilliun and I can be the dragon.' Then Tom started to prowl about Max and let out a yell as he pretended he was breathing out fire from his mouth. Max joined in with the game and pretended to attack the dragon with his sword. Tom ran off with Max running after him. After much running around the playground Tom found himself falling over a skipping rope that he hadn't noticed. He went crashing to the ground. Fortunately, he managed to stop his fall with his hands. He wanted to cry but knew he should not, as all the girls were standing around looking at him. Max helped his friend to his feet. Tom looked at his hands. They were badly scratched and blood was mixed with dirt.

'Oh dear, that looks sore!' said an unfamiliar voice. Both Max and Tom turned around to see the face of a girl who was very familiar to Max but he didn't remember seeing her in the school before. She was smaller than them and wore her hair in a plait that went a long way down her back. Her hair was a deep red colour and was tied with pink toggles. She was looking at Tom's hands and seemed very concerned.

'Yes ... it is a bit!' replied Tom, trying to hold back the tears.

'You should get it washed and have something put on it or you might get an infection,' said the girl, looking up into Tom's face.

'Yuk that does sound nasty. Maybe my hands will

31

turn black and fall off!' said Tom as he glared at his hands in horror.

Knowing that his friend was just trying to shock the girl, Max pulled Tom away saying 'Come on Tom, I think you'll live. Mrs Turner will have the first aid box, let's go find her.'

'Gotta go, eh what's your name?' said Max as he turned back to the girl.

The girl smiled. 'I'm Alicia. I'm in Mrs Green's class. It's my first day.'

'Hi, I'm Max and this is Tom. See you around.' The boys went off in search of Mrs Turner and Alicia stood watching for a while before going to join a couple of other girls.

Suddenly Max stopped. 'I don't believe it!' he exclaimed.

'What's up?' Tom asked.

'I've seen that girl before.'

'When? How?'

'She's the girl in my dreams. The one in the tower!' Max turned to look back across the playground but he could not spot her.

'Don't be silly. The picture of her is so small. You could not possibly know exactly what she looked like. It's a coincidence, that's all.'

'No. No, I'm sure it's her. I'm telling you it *is* her.' Max and Tom stared at each other. Then the whistle blew and they knew they had to get Tom's hands looked at before going into class.

That evening, Max examined the painting with his

magnifying glass. Tom was right; it was impossible to make out the girl's features in the painting. Max thought for a moment. Then he suddenly realised that just as he knew that the hero of the dreams was named Maximilliun, so too did he know what the girl looked like. He did not need the painting to tell him, for it was in his dreams. He put the painting back under his bed and felt happier. He didn't really know why, but he wasn't going to let it worry him. He went to bed that night with a feeling of peace.

6

Max or Maximilliun?

Max suddenly felt cold. He looked down and saw his wet clothes clinging to his body. He was very confused. He didn't know where he was. It looked like he was in a castle. Apart from the moon shining through a window, it was very dark. Max shook his head. 'I must be dreaming', he thought. Slowly, he remembered his dreams and went through all the events one by one. There was the dragon, the cellar and the old man with the white hair. He shivered as he thought about the huge spider. Then he remembered the girl with the lamp; the girl with the angelic face. Wind blew in from the window and made him shiver again.

'Oh no, I am Maximilliun!' he said out loud. His voice sounded strange and echoed back at him. This time, Max wasn't just watching the hero, somehow he really had become him. This time, he was able to think and feel like a real person. He felt that there was only one way to make sure and he pinched himself. 'Ow, that hurt,' he said out loud. 'It's true – I'm in my dream. Wow, I can't wait to tell Tom.'

Just then there was a strange sound from outside. He went over to the window and looked out at the terrifying beast below. Dakas looked about the size of four buses. He was throwing out long flames from his jaws and Max watched in horror as he saw a boy getting dangerously close. The boy was dressed in school uniform; Max felt his heart jump as he realised that the boy was Tom! Max stood completely still as he watched Tom jump back out of the reach of the dragon and run like he had never run before. Then the dragon flapped his wings and flew into the air – Max was desperate to help but didn't know how. Then he remembered how the river had saved him and knew that he had to tell his friend before it was too late.

'Tom! Tom! The river... the river behind you! Run Tom, run!' For a split second, Max was not sure whether Tom had heard him as the dragon was making such a noise as his wings beat the air. Max could see that the dragon was about to shoot out his fiery weapons at Tom but then everything seemed to happen at once. Tom turned and ran in the direction of the river, the dragon spat out flames and Max heard the sound of footsteps in the corridor behind him. Max knew that it was the old man with the beard. He was relieved to hear the footsteps moving quickly away from him but at the same time he was afraid for Tom, who now not only had a dragon to contend with, but also the old man.

As Max watched the scene outside the castle, he was relieved to see that Tom had just reached the river as the flames shot out above his head. Smoke rose up from the water and Max could not see his friend. The dragon had landed by the water's edge and stood looking down. As Max rushed out of the room and along the corridor, he was not sure whether he would be able to help, but he knew that he'd have to try.

The water felt really cold as Tominska jumped into the river.

He held his breath as he sank down deep. He was aware that Dakas' deadly flames had only just missed him. As he touched the bottom of the river, he could see the light from the dragon's fire above his head. Immediately he began to swim downstream, keeping well below the surface of the water. When he felt his lungs would burst through lack of air, he resurfaced. He gasped as his head came out of the water. He was pleased to see that he had managed, accidentally, to find the ideal place to hide amongst some reeds. Dakas had settled down some distance up-stream. Tominska decided to stay and tread water for a while, so that he could get his breathing back to normal.

Dakas looked all around but could not see his enemy. The dragon was relieved that this time, he had not been drenched with water. This meant that his fire hadn't been put out and he waited patiently to strike again. Dakas was prepared to wait all night if he had to. Then a voice was heard calling to the dragon; it was the old man. Tominska didn't hear what was being said but was surprised to see Dakas turn away from the riverside. His wings spread out and began to beat the air. Tominska watched, fascinated, as the dragon flew off. He breathed a sigh of relief.

It was at this moment that Max reached the front door of the castle. He hid behind the door and watched the dragon fly away. The old man just stood watching, too. Max was puzzled; why had the dragon flown away and where was Tom? He didn't have time to find out as he saw the old man was coming back to the castle. Max fled back along the corridor and hid behind a pillar. He held his breath as the old man's footsteps got closer. After what seemed like forever, he stopped very close to Max and made an odd noise; it sounded like a strange laugh but it could have been a grunt. Then he turned

36

around and went along another corridor. Max did not dare to breathe until the sound of the footsteps had faded away.

Max was worried about Tom. He hoped that the dragon had not reached his friend before he got to the river. Then he suddenly remembered that Tom couldn't swim! Max began to shake. This time it was not because of the cold, but from fear. He was afraid that Tom had drowned. He started back towards the door at the front of the castle – Max had to go and find out what had happened to his friend.

When he reached the door, he was alarmed to see that it was closed. He was afraid that it had been locked, because the key was in the door and it was much too high for Max to reach. He looked around to see if there was anything for him to climb on. To his delight, he found an old dusty wooden bench. Max tried to lift the bench. Then he tried to drag it along. Both of these methods failed and Max sat on the stone floor fighting back the tears that threatened to spill from his eyes. The tears blurred his vision and he blinked hard as he saw a white figure coming towards him. The figure was very tall and appeared to be jumping rather than running. Max felt his heart hammering in his chest. Then the figure passed him, unlocked the door and disappeared out into the darkness. Max blinked again as he thought the figure said 'I'm late, I'm late, for a very important date!' He pinched himself, as he was sure he was dreaming this time. Again, he felt the pain and winced. He rubbed his eyes to clear the tears away. Max rushed through the castle door and having checked for signs of the dragon, he dashed towards the river. Then everything went dark. He was still running but he could barely see anything.

*   *   *

Max felt hot and realised that his duvet was covering his head. His feet, on the other hand, felt cold. He pushed the quilt away and sat up. It had all been a dream, he thought. Then he realised his arm hurt and he pulled up his pyjama sleeve. On his arm were two dark bruises; so it had not been just a dream, it was real! Or perhaps he could have caused the bruises himself whilst asleep, because it felt so real at the time. He was happy to accept this thought when he noticed his hands, which looked quite grubby and when he turned them over to see the palms, they were covered in dust. The night before, he had had a bath and there was no way that they could have got dirty just lying in bed. It must have happened when he tried to pull that bench. Max was feeling very confused.

Max rushed out of bed and pulled out the painting. His eyes widened and his mouth dropped open as he saw the scene before him. The dragon was nowhere to be seen. The castle took up most of the picture with Maximilliun running just outside the large front door. The girl stood by the window in the tower just as before. What shocked Max was a figure just going round the corner of the castle. It was a white rabbit, as tall as a man, holding up a pocket watch. Max was completely astounded to think that the tall white figure that had passed him by was a rabbit. No wonder it seemed to be hopping, he thought.

Max searched the painting for signs of Tom but he could see none. He got out his magnifying glass and searched frantically. Eventually, something caught his eye. He was sure that what he saw amongst the trees was a shadowy figure. It had to be Tom, Max decided. Max slowly pushed the painting back under his bed. The adventure had not finished after all. He just couldn't wait to get to school and tell Tom all about it.

Max arrived at school very early as he was so excited and desperate to tell Tom all that had happened. Max was disappointed that his friend hadn't arrived and it was a full ten minutes before he saw the familiar blond-haired boy come rushing into the playground. If Max had not been so distracted, he would have noticed how untidy his friend looked. Tom ran to him shouting 'Max, you'll never guess!' At the same time Max said 'The dreams have come back!' They stood there looking at each other. 'What did you say?' Tom asked.

'The dreams have come back!' Max answered before he remembered his manners and said 'What was it you were going to say?'

'Well, it's really funny you have your dreams back, because I had a dream too!'

'What sort of dream?' asked Max, impatient to tell Tom all about his own dream.

'That's the odd thing, it was like your dreams. I suppose it was because of us talking about it yesterday. It was all about a castle and going to help Maximilliun rescue the girl from the tower. Then there was a dragon and it was chasing me.'

'The dragon was chasing you?'

'Yes. I mean no... I don't know. It was a boy

called Tominska.' Tom stood looking at Max with a puzzled expression on his face.

'But that's amazing! And did the dragon go after you, I mean Tominska? Did you hear me – I mean Maximilliun – shout for you to go into the river?'

'Yes, that's what happened. I – I mean Tominska – jumped into the river and swam under the water. Then the dragon stood by the riverbank waiting for me. Then a man with a white beard talked to the dragon and it flew away. I – or Tominska – climbed up the bank and hid behind a tree.'

'You really aren't sure whether it was you in the dream, or this boy called Tominska, are you?'

'I'm so confused. I really can't tell.'

'The same thing happened to me!' Max told Tom that during the dream he could feel and think normally and that he had pinched himself to test it out. Then he explained the whole of his dream to his friend and what he discovered when he woke up. The boys were silent for a while. Then Max said; 'You said that the boy in your dreams dived under the water and you don't swim, Tom.'

'That's true, I hadn't thought of that! So maybe I just want to be in the dream. But it felt so real!' Then a whistle screeched out and forced them to stop their discussion.

7

The White Rabbit

Max and Tom puzzled over the dreams all that day.
Every chance they had, they talked about it but
couldn't work out what had really happened. It was
later in the afternoon before Max remembered
something that he hadn't told Tom. It was at the
end of the lunchtime break when it came to him.

'Tom, I forgot to tell you about the rabbit!'

'What rabbit?' asked Tom, obviously having no idea
what his friend was talking about.

'The white rabbit. It had a pocket watch and it
talked...'

'You're talking about the rabbit from *Alice in
Wonderland*?' broke in Alicia, who had arrived without
them noticing. Both the boys turned to look at her.

'That's right,' replied Max nervously. 'We were just
saying it was a white rabbit, wasn't it? It wasn't a
brown one, was it?' Max hoped he sounded like he
knew what he was talking about.

'No, it's definitely a white rabbit. It's in my book
and it's one of my favourite pop-out books. I've read
it a million times. It also has a mad hatter and a
queen of hearts in it. You must have read it?'

'I don't think I have. It's that good, is it?'

'Well, I wouldn't have read it a million times if I didn't think so, now would I?'

'No of course not,' he replied. He was starting to think this girl was a mad hatter herself and was wishing Tom would say something so that they could get away.

Luckily for Max Alicia took her attention away from him and spoke to Tom. 'So you've read it then Tom?'

Tom knew he had to think quickly. He had not read the book and did not want Alicia to know what he and Max had been talking about.

'It's something we're doing in class. You know ... talking about different books and things. I haven't read the book but I think it was Jody said she had. That's right, isn't it Max?' Tom looked at his friend and hoped he wouldn't let him down. Max had realised what he was trying to do.

'Well it might have been Jody or it could have been Rosie. I can't really remember now. It was a white rabbit, I remember that bit now.' The boys glanced at each other but Alicia was not going to be fooled so easily. She sensed that there was something going on that she didn't know about.

'So it was Jody or Rosie who read the book then?' she asked. The boys glanced at each other again and then nodded their heads.

'I don't know who Jody or Rosie are,' Alicia continued, 'Perhaps you could point them out to me as I would love to have a chat with them about it. They must like the same books as me so perhaps

42

they can suggest other books I might like.' Alicia stood waiting for a reply. She was pleased to see the two boys looked uneasy.

'Er... yes,' replied Max 'I think you might have to wait though because they're off sick at the moment.' Max smiled at his own quickness of thought.

'Chickenpox, I heard. Or it could have been measles,' added Tom.

'I see,' smiled Alicia. 'I'm sure I will be able to catch up with them soon though. Chickenpox or measles, you said?'

'It could have been both. I don't remember now. Do you know, Max?'

Max looked very uncomfortable and muttered, 'Sorry, I don't know.' Alicia turned away from the boys, went a few paces and then turned back. 'I'll catch up with Jody and Rosie when they get back. I could do with a couple of good, honest friends.' Then she tossed her ponytail and ran off.

Max looked at Tom. 'What did you have to say they had chickenpox or measles for?'

'If Alicia thinks they're going to be off a long time, she might forget all about it in a week or two.'

'She might have done if you hadn't made it sound so unbelievable. Isn't it funny that Alicia is identical to the girl in the tower?' The boys stood looking at each other for a few seconds. Then Max said; 'Anyway this *Alice in...*, where was it now?'

'Wonderland, *Alice in Wonderland*. You must have heard of it! I haven't read it though, it's a girls' book.'

'I wonder if there's a copy in the library. We'll

43

have to have a look.' The boys walked side by side back across the playground. They knew that the whistle would soon be going and lunchtime was nearly over.

Max and Tom had to wait until the end of school before they could make their way to the library. There was no one around when they went in and it took them a full five minutes before they found what they were looking for.

'Here it is,' called Tom to his friend. Max went over to him and grabbed the book from his hands.

'*Alice in Wonderland* by Lewis Carroll,' he read as he flicked through the pages. There were a few pictures in the book and Max found one with a tall white rabbit in it. It had on a little waistcoat and was looking down at a pocket watch in its paw. Max stared at the picture. 'It's just like the one in the painting. That's really odd. How could I possibly have a white rabbit in my dream just like the one in this book? I swear I've never seen this before.'

'Maybe you did when you were very young. Maybe when you were only three or four, your mum read it to you. We never remember things like that, do we? I mean, not properly. Probably we just sort of store it in our heads and then we dream and out it pops.' Max considered this idea, closed the book and gave it back to Tom.

'You know, I think you might be right there, Tom,' he said with a smile on his face. Tom was pleased that he had helped his friend with this problem. He grinned back at Max and put the book back onto the shelf.

The boys rushed out of the library and went home feeling quite happy. They both knew that there were still a lot of unanswered questions but they were content that they had found a solution to at least one.

Max realised that he had reached the riverbank. He stood listening for a moment. He was sure Tom was somewhere nearby. All he could hear was the sound of water moving. He thought he could see a figure in the distance and leaned over to look more closely.

'Hi, young man!' The voice came from behind and Max nearly fell into the river with the shock of it. He steadied himself and then turned to see the old man standing in front of him. He could not see the expression on his face, as the light of the moon was behind him. Max felt trapped as the man seemed so big. He was just thinking that it would be best to jump into the river, when suddenly there was a rushing sound from behind the old man, who turned to see what the noise was. Max was not going to let the same curiosity stop him from taking the opportunity to make his escape.

'Hey, you there, come back!' called the man, but Max did not slow down for a moment. He stumbled several times along the way but each time he continued on, trying to get as far away as he could. He eventually found himself in a thick forest where it was difficult to move too quickly. After a further few minutes Max came to a standstill. He could hardly breathe and trickles of sweat were running down his face. He felt so hot and tired, he had to sit down on a thick log to rest.

Max felt like a coward. He had not stood up for himself but had just run away. He had no idea where Tom was and now he had got himself lost in a forest, where it was very dark and there were strange noises around him. Max put his head in his hands and started to cry.

'You must be feeling very sad,' said a sweet, small voice. Max stopped crying and looked up. He was surprised that in front of him was a bright light. He blinked his eyes several times. Then he could see that the light was in fact a very small figure dressed in white. The figure had the most beautiful tissue paper-thin wings, which moved so fast that leaves on the forest floor were being tossed up into the air. There was the most amazing smell, like roses, vanilla ice cream and strawberries all mixed together. He just stared at the figure because he didn't know what else to do.

'Are you feeling better now?'

'I ... I ... yes thank you,' replied Max. Things had not really changed for he had still deserted his friend. However, he did feel better.

'Are you ... I mean ... are you a fairy?' he asked quietly.

'Yes, I'm your fairy!'

'My fairy? I didn't know I had one.'

The little fairy laughed and it was an odd sound. Max thought it sounded like the chimes his mum had put in the garden.

'Why were you crying?' the fairy asked.

'I came to rescue the girl in the tower. I fell in the river whilst I was trying to get away from Dakas the Dragon. Then I got into the castle and I nearly got eaten by a giant spider. Then I saw my friend Tom being chased by Dakas, so I rushed out to help him. Then the old man came and I got scared and I ran away.' At this point of the story Max nearly

46

burst out crying, but the fairy waved a wand and stars of silver and gold bounced around him. Max was fascinated to watch them as they shone so brightly.

'That is a lot of "thens", isn't it?' Max did not feel he needed to answer this question, so he didn't. 'I shouldn't worry about your friend Tom, he is doing just fine. You have already shown how brave you are and you will finish this dream.'

'What do you mean "finish this dream"?' Max asked. Then, all of a sudden, a bright light shone through the trees just behind him and he turned to see what it was. It was the sun rising above the trees – Max thought that it had become morning very quickly. He turned back to the fairy but she had gone. For a second, he wondered if he had imagined it all but then he heard that wonderful laughter again. He smiled as six or seven golden stars seemed to dance before him and faded leaving a lovely smell of roses, vanilla ice cream and strawberries.

8

The Boys Share Their Dreams

Max woke with a shiver. He realised that he was quite damp and indeed when he felt his pyjamas, they were wet. 'It must have been all that running,' he thought. Then he realised that it was strange that he was now not surprised that his dreams were becoming more and more real to him. He pulled off his pyjamas, wrapped himself in his dressing gown and drew the painting out from under the bed. He looked at the painting and smiled. Everything was all right; the fairy had told him the truth. He pushed his feet into his slippers and went down for breakfast. Max wanted to get to school to tell Tom all about his dream and to find out if Tom had anything to report.

Both boys arrived at school a full twenty minutes earlier than usual. They were both bursting with news for each other.

'Tom, I've had another dream! What about you?'

'Yes ... it was amazing! I shall tell you all about it in a minute but first I have to tell you – I was all wet this morning!'

'All wet, what ... you mean everything?'

'Yes, my pyjamas, my bed and my hair. Try explaining that one to your mum!'

'Wow! That was because you went into the river. And you went completely under the water...'

'So it must mean I'm really in this adventure! So I am Tominska!' Both boys stood staring at one another not knowing what to make of it all.

'Tell me what happened in your dream. I'm dying to know as I didn't see you in my dream at all, but the fairy told me you were all right,' asked Max.

'The fairy? What fairy?'

'Look, just tell me your story first.'

'Oh, all right. Now, let me see... It started when I realised I was really cold. I was shivering.'

'Hey, that's what happened to me the night before last!'

'It's a very odd feeling, isn't it? It seemed like a dream, but it wasn't.'

'I know exactly what you mean. So did you try pinching yourself?'

'No I did not! Do you think I'm that silly?' Max gave Tom an angry look.

'Sorry, I'm only joking. No, to be honest I didn't think about it. I suppose I was too busy worrying about the dragon and the old man. I found myself hiding behind a tree. Then I spotted you a little way down by the river and I was just going to call out when I saw the old man coming up behind you.'

'You saw us both? So why didn't you help me, then?'

'Well, that's gratitude for you! Why do you think he looked round?'

'You mean you made that funny noise?'

'Frightening, don't you think?' said Tom as he crossed his arms and stuck his nose in the air.

'I'm not sure I would call it frightening but it was certainly an odd sound.'

'Thank you very much! I won't bother to help you again,' replied Tom sulkily.

'Look, I didn't mean that. It was a very clever thing to do and it did help me to escape. So come on – tell me what happened to the old man.'

Tom was pleased that Max appreciated his distraction plan. 'I could see you dashing off and for a moment the man didn't know whether to follow you or come after me. As soon as I realised he was coming for me, I ran like the wind!'

'Where did you go?'

'At first I ran in the opposite direction, back towards the castle. Then I remembered that the dragon was probably that way, so I turned back. I would have been happy to fight the dragon, but then I realised that I didn't have my sword with me...'

'Your sword?' Max interrupted. 'What sword?'

'I don't know, do I? I just remembered I didn't have it. So I couldn't fight the dragon. I managed to ram right into the man and sent him flying. Then I tried to follow you but you had gone by that time.'

'I ran into a very dark forest. I was upset because I didn't know that you had escaped. I thought you'd drowned!'

'So how did you get out of the forest?'

'How do you know I got out of the forest?'

'The rabbit told me.'

'What, you mean the *Alice in Wonderland* rabbit?'

'Yes. We had quite a chat, really.'

'You had a chat with a six-foot rabbit?'

'Yes. He was a bit scatty, I can tell you that. He seemed to be more interested in not being late. What for, I never did find out.'

'I'll tell you what, Tom, this is one strange adventure. If it was only me then I might be just going loony, but with you having the same story going on in your dreams...'

'I know. It is a bit weird, isn't it?'

There were a lot of other children running around now in the playground and both boys felt that it was now too crowded to continue their talk.

'I'll tell you about the fairy later, okay?' whispered Max. Tom just nodded. They stood side by side, both remembering their dreams from the previous night. No one seemed to take any notice of them, except Alicia. She was standing quite a way off but she could see that there was a look of excitement on the boys' faces. She wished she could share their secret. It made her feel quite alone.

At playtime, the boys found a quiet spot to continue their conversation. Max told Tom all about his encounter with the fairy and Tom told Max how he had seen him coming out of the forest. Tom was very concerned that he didn't know where his sword was. He felt sure he should. Max told his friend what the painting had looked like in the morning. He explained that the castle was quite small in the picture, which mostly showed the edge of the wood, with the sun coming up behind it. At one side of the painting there stood Tom. That was how he had known that his friend hadn't drowned.

The boys had a good day, despite maths, because they were so looking forward to the next dream. They both felt that together, they would be able to get back into the castle and rescue the girl in the tower.

Their last lesson that day was football. They did a lot of warming-up exercises, mostly going round cones. After that they had a match against the girls. The previous week the girls had beaten them three goals to one and they were determined that was not going to happen again. The boys won, mostly by fair means, by two goals to nil. There were a lot of jokes about girls not playing proper football and last week just being a fluke. So both Max and Tom were in happy spirits when the lesson came to an end. They dawdled behind the rest and were just going into the changing rooms when they heard their names being called.

'Hey, you boys! Tom and Max, isn't it?' called a large man whom Max recognised as being the new caretaker.

'Yes?' replied Max.

'I wonder if you wouldn't mind helping me to clear away these things. I have to rush off in a minute and when I get back it will be quite dark. I wouldn't normally ask, but you look like helpful boys to me. It'll only take a minute.' The man stood looking over some round-framed glasses at the boys. They both felt he had asked so kindly that they could not refuse his request, so they rushed about collecting all the cones and stray balls that had been scattered around the pitch. Once the job was done, they waved goodbye to the man who waved back and said 'Thank you, Max. Thank you, Tom. Sweet dreams!'

They were back inside the school before Tom turned to Max and said 'Hang on, how does he know our names?'

Max pushed his hand through his hair and shook his head. 'I don't know. He's only been at the school a couple of weeks. How would he know our names?'

'And, what was that bit about sweet dreams? There's something fishy about him.'

'I know this is freaky, but does he remind you of the man in our dreams?' asked Max.

'No – surely not! It can't be. He doesn't have a white beard.' The boys had no chance to continue their conversation as they were with the other children again. Tom's mum had come to pick them up from school and there were no more opportunities to talk further about this strange turn of events.

9

The Painting Disappears

Max went back to Tom's house for an hour after
school because his mum had gone to London with
his Auntie Clare to visit an art exhibition. Max could
not understand why she should be doing such a
boring thing, but then mums could be very strange
at times he thought. Both boys would have loved to
talk about this new development in the adventure
but could not – Tom had two sisters and one toddler
brother and the house was just not big enough for
the two friends to find a quiet spot. They had to be
content to munch biscuits in front of the television.
Tom's mum seemed to spend much of her time getting
little Charlie out of things he should not be in to.
Tom's sisters spent most of their time arguing and
Flossie the cat kept trying to climb onto Max. Max
was glad when his mum called for him and took
him home to a peaceful house.

Max ran upstairs to change out of his school
uniform. He put on a T-shirt and some jeans. He
was just about to go downstairs when he suddenly
thought about the painting. Max knelt down by his
bed and looked underneath. He gasped – it was gone!

Max's heart beat faster. Where could it have gone, he asked himself? Either it had simply disappeared or else Mum had taken it. He reasoned that she would be the only one to come into his room. He rushed down the stairs. Then he suddenly realised that he could not ask her about the painting. She would know that the only way he would have it there would be because he had taken it from the loft. Max didn't know what to do.

'Hi, Sunshine, dinner won't be long. We're having quiche – would you like beans or salad? Dad won't be home till late so we'll get on and have ours,' called Mum from the kitchen. Max wandered into the kitchen just as his mum turned from the fridge.

As there was no reply Mum tried again. 'Max! Make your mind up. Which would you like?'

'I, I don't mind, Mum,' replied Max in a quiet voice.

Max's mum stopped what she was doing and looked at him. 'Everything all right, Max?' she asked.

'Fine. It's just that I thought I left something underneath my bed but it's not there,' replied Max, hoping that he had not reminded his mum about the painting. Fortunately, her expression didn't change.

'What was it, Max? I took the vacuum cleaner in there today but I didn't notice anything. Apart, that is, from those pyjama bottoms that went missing last week. I found them underneath your bed.' Max had to try not to be surprised at this bit of strange news. As he struggled to look normal, however, he seemed to have lost his power of speech. Mother and son stood looking at each other. Eventually, Mum broke the silence. 'Well Max, was it something important?'

'No, no ... not really. It's just a comic that Tom lent me and I said I would give it back tomorrow.' Mum smiled and went to turn the oven on.

'Mum?'

'Yes?'

'My pyjama bottoms? Were they all right? I mean, they weren't ... they were okay?'

'Yes, Max, they were fine. Why, is there a problem?'

'No, I ... I just don't remember leaving them there, that's all.' Max dashed into the lounge and punched the air. He felt like laughing out loud. He just couldn't believe that somehow, some way, his pyjama bottoms had just turned up out of the blue. He was still smiling at how amazing this adventure was when his mum came into the room. She saw the look on her son's face but couldn't make it out. 'You're sure you're all right, Max? There's nothing troubling you, is there? No problems at school, bullying or teachers you're not getting on with?' Max had shaken his head at each of these questions. Mum lifted her eyebrows, said 'Okay' and left to prepare their dinner.

Max turned on the television and flopped onto the sofa. He wished that his mum and dad would let him have a mobile phone. He really wanted to talk to Tom. There was nothing he wanted to watch on the television, so he went upstairs to put on the computer in the spare room. Max's mum found him engrossed in a game when she looked in to tell him dinner was on the table. 'I decided to do beans and salad,' she said as she smiled down at him. However, her smile did not betray her worries about Max and she decided she would talk to his dad later...

Max slept fitfully that night. Mum had to call him three times to get him to even open his eyes the next morning. Max was not at all surprised that he had not dreamt the usual dream. Instead he had a strange dream about some pyjama bottoms. They had been so big that when he put them on, they went up to his chin. They had pictures of dragons on them. Then suddenly all the dragons came to life and jumped off the pyjamas. They flew around puffing out large flames. Eventually the pyjamas burnt up and Max looked down to see that his legs were burnt bright red. Then he had woken up.

When Max opened his eyes, he knew that he ought to get out of bed but he didn't want to. He thought that perhaps he could complain of a bad throat. Maybe Mum would let him stay in bed. He was just thinking what a good idea that was, when he noticed something strange on the ceiling by the wardrobe, like something on top of it was reflecting onto the ceiling. Max became very curious. He got out of bed and pulled his chair across the room. He stood on the chair and reached up.

'Max! I hope you're out of bed now, or you'll be in trouble, my boy!' shouted Mum from downstairs.

'Yes... I'm up, Mum. I'll be down in two secs!' answered Max.

Max felt something cold and smooth on top of the wardrobe. Then, as if someone had suddenly turned on a light, Max knew what he was touching. The reflection on the ceiling had been made by a mirror. It was a painting in a mirrored frame. It was THE painting! Max felt along the edge and was going to pull it down when he realised that he would never be strong enough to lift it on his own. He felt frustrated. There was only one thing for it; he would have to get Tom to help him. He jumped off the chair and went downstairs for breakfast.

Despite Max being late getting up, he still managed to get to school before Tom that morning. He was standing just inside the school gates watching for his friend. While he was waiting, he suddenly realised that there was someone standing just behind him. He looked round to see Alicia smiling up at him.

'Hello Max, looking for Tom?' she asked.

'Yeah, he seems to be a bit late today.' Max continued to look up the road in the hope that Alicia would not want to stay and talk to him.

'You're best mates, aren't you?' Alicia continued.

'Yeah, we've been mates since forever.'

'It must be good to have someone you can share your secrets with. I never seem to stay in one place long enough to make friends like that.'

Max didn't really want to let Tom catch him speaking to a girl but he couldn't help being curious. 'Why do you move around so much then? Is it your dad's job?'

'No. I don't have a dad or a mum.' Max turned to look at Alicia and was surprised to see that she didn't look particularly upset.

'It doesn't worry you not having parents, then?'

'Sometimes it does, but I was only a baby when they died. I've had lots of foster parents and they've been really good to me. Sometimes I think it would be good to have a mum and dad you could live with all the time, then maybe I'd stay in a town long enough to have friends like you and Tom.'

Max felt very sorry for this little girl and if she had not been a girl, he would have asked her to be his friend. So instead he said; 'I expect you'll settle down one day,' but he knew that he didn't sound very convincing.

At that moment, the whistle blew and Tom came running through the school gates.

10

Max and Tom Work Together

The morning seemed endless to the two boys. They were so desperate to talk about their adventures. When eventually morning break came they rushed off to find a quiet corner of the playground. Tom was quite relieved that Max hadn't had a dream either. Max explained all about the painting having gone missing, then appearing on top of his wardrobe and about his pyjama bottoms having suddenly come back. Tom didn't know what to say. All he could come up with was 'I'm flabbergasted!' It was a word that he had just come across and he felt sure it was a good time to say it.

'So,' said Max, 'what do you think about the caretaker? Do you think he is our bearded man – I mean, without the beard, or what?'

'He did seem familiar to me too. But surely he can't be our man... I mean, how is he in our dreams?'

'The more I think about it, the more I'm convinced. I was talking to Alicia this morning...'

'Yes, I noticed that,' Tom interrupted. 'Don't tell me she was going on about *Alice in Wonderland* again!'

'No, thankfully it looks like she's forgotten about

that. I hope so, anyway. Now I've forgotten what I was going to say. Oh yes, I remember now – the more I see Alicia, the more I think she reminds me of the girl in the tower.'

'I don't know about that. I haven't really seen the girl in the tower, have I?'

'It's so odd. It is true that I've seen the caretaker before the dreams started, but I really don't think I had seen Alicia before. What I mean to say is, you can dream about people you have already met, but I'm sure you can't dream about people you haven't met.' Max looked at Tom to see if he agreed with this thought. Several seconds went by as Tom looked like he was thinking hard. Then he said 'I'm just flabbergasted, I really am.'

'Tom, that is not at all helpful, you know.'

'I can't help it. I'm just flabbergasted.'

'Would you just stop saying that!' Max replied, pushing Tom gently on the arm.

'Here, if you're not careful I will get onto my flying dragon and attack you!' Tom stretched out his arms, pushed his head forward and dived at Max. Max turned to run away. 'You can't catch me! I'm a knight in shining armour and my horse is as fast as the wind!' By this time, Max had sped off with Tom chasing behind him. The boys were so intent on their game that they forgot all about their real-life adventure for the time being.

That afternoon when Max got home, he went straight up to his bedroom. He automatically looked up to the top of the wardrobe, but the painting had gone. Panic took hold of him for a couple of seconds, until he thought to look under his bed. He touched something cold. Max drew the painting out into the room. He was relieved that he hadn't had to wait until he could have Tom round to help him get it down from the wardrobe.

Max sat back on his heels and stared down at the painting. It looked almost the same as before, except for one thing; standing beside the figure of Tom was Max. A smile spread over his face and he just couldn't wait for the next dream. He hoped that it would be that night. At that moment, he heard his mum coming up the stairs and he pushed the painting back into its hiding place.

The evening went much too slowly for Max and he was quite pleased when it was eight o'clock so that he could go up to bed. Something told him that tonight would be the night! When he eventually snuggled down into his duvet, he suddenly remembered the caretaker's parting words: 'Sweet dreams'! Within minutes he was asleep ... or was he?

One minute Tom was all alone and the next Max was there beside him. Tom jumped slightly and said 'Hey, where did you just spring from?'

'I think I was just asleep in my bed and now I'm here. I'm sorry if I gave you a fright but really I have no control over this any more than you do! Anyway, before I went to bed I saw the painting and we were standing just like this, together...'

'What painting?' Tom asked.

'What do you mean, "what painting?" Surely you know what I'm talking about, Tom?'

'Tominska, if you don't mind,' Tom said. Max stood staring at Tom for a moment. Then he noticed a twinkle in his friend's eye, followed by a slight twitch at the edge of his lips.

'You ... you toad you!' said Max as Tom started to chuckle.

'Got you going there, didn't I?' laughed Tom. Max grinned and pushed his friend. 'Look you, this is serious, we're here to rescue the girl in the tower, so stop messing about. That dragon is around here somewhere, you know!'

'He wasn't in the painting, then? Hey, I thought the painting was on top of your wardrobe?'

'When I got in from school, I found it under my bed again. And no, before you ask, I don't think my mum put it there. This adventure gets weirder by the minute. I couldn't see the dragon in the painting but it does seem to appear from nowhere, so we'd better go carefully.'

Max turned back towards the castle with Tom following closely behind him. The door to the castle was closed. The handle was well out of their reach and they decided that Tom should climb up onto Max's shoulders to open the door. Tom found he could just reach the handle and prayed desperately that the door was not locked. The handle was heavy and stiff, so that Tom needed both hands to turn it. He was finding it very difficult as he was wobbling badly, but eventually the door gave way and Tom fell forward on to the floor. They made such a noise entering the castle that both the boys were afraid they had been heard. Max helped Tom to his feet and it seemed that he was unhurt by the fall.

'This way!' Max whispered. He led Tom up a stairway, all the time trying to move quickly and as quietly as he could. They came to the two passageways that Max had

63

reached before. Once again it was very dark. Max suddenly remembered his encounter with the spider and gave a little shudder. After a slight hesitation, he turned down the right-hand corridor.

'Max, do you know where we're going?' whispered Tom as he tried to keep up with his friend.

'Not really. There must be another staircase somewhere. We have to get to the top of the castle.' Then he stopped, for the corridor had come to an end. They turned back. Along the way they had passed a door. Somehow they both knew that they should go back and check out what was on the other side of it. They reached the room and stood either side of the door. They could just about see each other, as there was a small window opposite them. Max listened, but couldn't hear any sound coming from the room, so he put his hand on the door handle. Fortunately, this handle was only about head height. Tom nodded to Max to let him know that he was with him. Max turned the handle and rushed into the room with Tom right on his heels. They both stood still with their hearts pounding away. In front of them sat the man with the white beard.

Both boys noticed that there was a staircase in the corner of the room. The man stood up and started towards them, but Max and Tom didn't hear what he said because they had both turned around and dashed back down the dark corridor. They ran as fast as their legs would carry them. They soon reached the staircase once more. The boys seemed to fly down the stairs and when they reached the bottom Tom grabbed Max by the shoulders.

'Look Max, I'll run on outside and try and draw the old man away. You hide somewhere and get back up stairs when he follows me. Okay?'

'Watch out for the dragon, Tom. You will be careful, won't you?'

'I'll be fine. Quickly – you must hide, he's coming. Go on, hide!' The boys went in opposite directions. Tom rushed out of the front door as noisily as he could. He left the door wide open. Max crept behind the pillar that he had so successfully hidden behind before. In less than five seconds, the man came puffing down the stairs. He stopped not far from Max and leaned forward with his hands on his knees. He struggled to get his breath back, while Max held his. After a while the man straightened up and went out through the door. Max, breathing a sigh of relief, made his way back up the stairs and on his way, he saw out of a small window. He stopped in his tracks. Below him he could see that not only had Tom come face to face with Dakas again, that would have been bad enough, but on top of that the old man was close behind him. Max didn't know what to do. He knew that however fast he ran he would not be able to reach his friend in time. Then he gasped as he saw Tom pull out a large shiny sword.

Tom was suddenly aware that he was trapped between the dragon and the old man. He pulled out his sword with confidence. Then he remembered that he hadn't had a sword just a few minutes ago. He thought that he must be dreaming and if that were so, he hoped he would wake up in his bed. He did not wake up in his bed. 'There's nothing for it,' he thought. 'I'll just have to fight!'

Tom ran straight towards Dakas the Dragon, who was ready to attack. When he got very close to the beast, he suddenly turned to the left. This quick movement had the effect of startling the dragon, who now had his mouth wide open. Dakas turned towards the attacker. Flames shot out at Tom – he just managed to escape, although he could feel the heat of the flames and this spurred him on.

Tom didn't know how he was going to keep the dragon busy without getting burnt to a crisp, but he knew that he needed to give Max as much time as possible to rescue the girl. As he was small, Tom had the advantage of being able to move quickly. The dragon was easily confused by Tom's tactics. The battle went on for some time, with Tom just managing to avoid the dragon's fiery assault. He had successfully managed to turn the beast around so that the dragon was between him and the old man. Every now and then Tom stabbed at Dakas with his sword, but each time the dragon moved out of its reach. Tom was getting very tired and knew that he could not keep up this fight for much longer. He turned back towards the dragon one more time and darted under the large green neck. Dakas could no longer see his enemy. Tom swung his sword through the air and hit the dragon in the throat. Dakas let out a terrible, earth shattering scream and began to sink down to the ground. Tom ran to escape being crushed by the huge body of the dragon. He thought he had got away, when suddenly the head of the beast came down heavily upon him. Everything went dark. He could not see or hear anything. As he drifted off into the deepest sleep he had ever known, Tom's only thought was that he wanted to wake up safely in his own bed.

11

Max Meets the Girl in the Tower

Max had been watching Tom and the dragon fearfully from the window of the castle. Suddenly, he heard a door bang from below and it seemed to wake him up. He realised that Tom was putting his life at risk to enable him to rescue the girl. Max fled along the corridor, into the room where they had previously met the old man and climbed quickly up the stairs. It was a spiral staircase, quite narrow and very dark, which made Max shiver with fear. This was made worse by the occasional spider's web that brushed his face. He tried hard to keep his mind on rescuing the girl as he went round and round the ascending stairs.

After some time, he could see a faint light and realised he must be near the top. By now he was quite breathless and just managed to struggle up the last few steps. At the top there was a well-lit passageway where he stopped for a few seconds to get his breath back and as he did so, he could hear music. Max followed the sound of the music into a large room. Straight in front of him was a large bed and above the bed hung a beautiful painting. It was of a forest scene, with little fairies dancing around a fire. The light from the fire was reflected on their faces. Each face, although different, looked so joyful that Max found it difficult to drag his attention away from it. Eventually he turned towards the source of the music. It was the girl singing. She was sitting at a dressing table, which was full of little ornaments and bottles of every colour of the rainbow. She didn't seem to realise he was there.

'Er ... excuse me,' began Max, awkwardly, 'I've come to rescue you.' The girl turned around slowly. She smiled at him and he smiled back. She continued to look at him and he didn't know what to do. All he could think of was that this girl was definitely Alicia.

'Don't you think we had better be going?' Max said at last. He went towards her and reached out his hand. The girl gave a little laugh.

'Look, we really do have to move quickly. Tom is keeping the dragon busy. I don't know where that old man's gone but I'm sure he'll be here any minute. We have to get away!' Still the girl didn't move. Max was just thinking about grabbing her by the arm and dragging her back down the stairs when she spoke at last.

'There really is no need for you to get so upset.'

'Upset! Upset! Of course I'm getting upset! My friend is putting his life at risk so that I can save you. We have to hurry!' Max knew that his voice was getting louder and sounding crosser with every word, but he couldn't help it.

'Why on earth would you think I need saving!'

'Do you mean to say we've gone through all this trouble and you don't want to be saved? And by the way, my friend is out there right now trying to stop Dakas from frying him for breakfast!' Max was so angry that he had completely forgotten that his shouting could probably be heard throughout the whole castle.

They both stood staring at each other when suddenly a

sound came from the doorway. Max turned round quickly, drawing out his sword at the same time. 'Where did I get that from?' he thought, as he pointed it at the intruder. However, he lowered his sword as he realised it was the girl he had met with the pet spider. Then he raised it up again as he saw two large hairy legs enter the room.

'Crawler, go back downstairs. You will only frighten the poor boy,' called the girl. Max put his sword down again, but did not put it away. He wanted to have it ready, just in case.

'Look, can somebody tell me what this is all about?' Max asked looking from one girl to the other.

'We had hoped you would know. It is your dream after all!' answered the girl at the dressing table.

'Is it? Is it really a dream? I don't know any more,' Max said, shaking his head slowly with confusion. 'Perhaps if you tell me who you are it would help, and what about my friend Tom?'

'Your friend will be fine, you can rest assured about that. Have you ever heard of anyone really getting hurt in a dream?' Max stood, looking completely puzzled by this thought.

'Anyway, my name is Aliciana and this is Miss Gemima Muffet,' she continued.

'So you are Alicia then? I knew it!' replied Max.

'No, no! My name is Aliciana. I told you!' the girl said plainly.

'This is really bizarre. All right then, who is the man with the white beard? And, what about this Dakas?'

'The man with the white beard is Nicholas and Dakas is the dragon that protects me.'

'So the dragon is here to protect you? You mean, he is not keeping you here against your will then?'

'No of course not, what a silly thing to say!' chipped in

69

Gemima Muffet. She sat down on a soft chair beside the bed with her cream dress floating around her.

Max, ignoring Gemima, turned back to Aliciana and said, 'He has already tried to attack me and my friend Tom. Why would he want to kill us when we don't mean you any harm?'

'Well he didn't know that, did he? If only you had given Nicholas a chance to speak to you. Every time he caught up with you, you ran away.'

'I thought he was the one who had locked you away. Now I suppose you are going to tell me he's your friend?'

'Of course I am. He is everybody's friend!' Aliciana frowned at Max. 'You really shouldn't try to make out everyone is against you. Most people are really nice, you know.'

'I'm sorry, but this started off as just a dream. Then it suddenly became real. I'm beginning to think I should never have got the painting down from the loft.' Max slumped down into a chair next to Gemima.

'Oh the painting, yes, it is all in the painting you know,' said Aliciana. 'Come and have a look at it.' She turned back and seemed to be looking into the mirror in front of her. Max got up and stood looking over her shoulder. As he looked at the mirror he realised that the edge was identical to the picture frame that his painting was in. Then something very strange happened. As Max looked at the mirror it went hazy. Colours danced around it, but had no form. Eventually a picture began to take shape. It was exactly how Max had seen the painting the very first time. Max stood staring at the picture, as it changed with each dream he had experienced. In time the picture went back to just colours again. Several seconds passed by, then it cleared and Max could see a picture of a girl in her bedroom. The girl looked very sad. 'Wow!' he said as the face became clear. 'That's Alicia!'

'Yes, you're right, that is Alicia. She is the one that needs rescuing,' replied Aliciana. As Max continued to look into the picture of Alicia, his vision started to go blurred. Then all of a sudden, his knees collapsed beneath him and he fell to the floor.

Then Max woke up.

12

Max is Confused

Max woke up feeling very tired. He felt hot and cold all over. His hair was stuck to his forehead with sweat. The dream seemed very vivid and he felt a sense of fear, but didn't know why. Then he heard his mum calling him to get up. He tried to sit up but needed to use all his energy to manage it.

It was some time later that Max's mum went in to his room. She took one look at him and gently pushed him back into bed. She covered him up with his quilt and felt his forehead. 'You're staying right there, my boy,' she said.

'I feel awful, Mum...' croaked Max.

'Yes, I'm not surprised. You look terrible. I'll get you some tablets and a nice hot drink. I won't be a minute, Pet.' Mum kissed him on his hot brow and went off. Max dozed. Some five minutes later, Max's mum found him fast asleep. When she tried to rouse him and he could not be woken, her heart skipped a beat. She rushed to phone the doctor's surgery and was immediately transferred to Dr Simmons. As the doctor spoke so calmly, she felt her panic subside. He told her to get some damp flannels and put them on Max. He said that it sounded like his temperature had risen too much and that she must try to bring it down. Dr Simmons was keen for her to phone back after about ten minutes to let him know how things were. Mum followed the doctor's instructions and felt better now that she was able to do something to help Max.

In Tom's house a similar scene was taking place. Tom's mum had found her son on the floor beside his bed. He was completely unconscious and had a raging fever. His mum had lost no time and phoned for an ambulance straight away. As soon as the ambulance arrived, they wasted no time in getting Tom onto a stretcher. They were saying very reassuring things to his mum while quickly sliding the stretcher into the ambulance. The ambulance sped through the town with the siren going. Once or twice Tom groaned, but he stayed unconscious. His mum sat holding his hand and praying that her son would be all right.

Max opened his eyes. Aliciana was one side of him and Gemima was on the other. 'What happened?' he asked.

'You fainted, that's what happened!' replied Aliciana gently. 'Maybe what you saw in the mirror gave you a shock. Are you feeling better now? You still look a little pale.'

'Yes, I'm fine thank you,' Max insisted.

'Perhaps we should get him onto the chair?' suggested Gemima.

'I think you're right. Come on Max, up you come,' said Aliciana as she took his arm. Gemima took hold of his other arm. Max struggled to stand up and found that he needed the girl's help. 'Ouch... My head hurts!' groaned Max.

'Well, I'm not surprised!' replied Aliciana. 'You caught your head on the edge of my chair as you fell. You've got a nasty gash. We should clean it up before you get an infection.' Max had a feeling he had heard those words before somewhere.

By this time, the girls had managed to settle Max on the chair. Then they all looked towards the door as the sound of footsteps on the stairs drew their attention.

Max looked around for his sword but he couldn't see it. He tried to stand, but felt dizzy and sat back heavily onto the chair.

The door opened and in came Nicholas, with Tom in his arms. Tom was obviously unconscious and Max felt his heart thumping quickly in his chest.

'What have you done?' he shouted. Again he tried to stand, but the girls pushed him firmly back onto the chair.

'What have I done? I think you can only blame yourself for this tom-foolery!' replied Nicholas. 'If you two scallywags go around looking for trouble, you will probably find it.'

'Us, looking for trouble! What do you expect us to do when that hulking great dragon comes spitting fire at us?' Max had managed to stand up, despite the girls' efforts to keep him in the chair. He rushed over to the bed where Nicholas had laid Tom. Max touched Tom's forehead and felt the nasty bump that looked very pink and sore.

'Tom... Tom! Please speak to me, Tom...'

'He'll be all right in a bit; don't you go worrying now!' said Nicholas.

'That's all very well for you to say, but how do I know you're right?'

'Because it is just a dream,' answered Aliciana, standing beside him.

'You said that he couldn't get hurt because it's just a dream, but we have both got bumps on our heads and Tom is completely out of it!'

'Yes, I know I said that and it's true. In real life you will be fine.'

Max felt very confused – he didn't know whether it was because it was all very confusing or because he had a bump on his head. Tom groaned. Max went to him and spoke gently. Tom put his hand up to his forehead and said quite clearly 'Ouch ... my head hurts!' Max was so thrilled that his friend had woken up, he just hugged him.

'What are you doing? Get off me, Max!' Tom said as he struggled to sit up.

'You're all right then, Tom?'

'I'm fine, well ... apart from a lump on my head!' Tom touched his lump and grimaced. 'Hey, what happened to Dakas?'

'Oh, don't worry, he's fine!' replied Nicholas.

'So he's not dead then?'

'I do hope not.'

'Look, I don't understand what's going on here...'

'You're not the only one,' replied Max. Nicholas and Gemima looked at Aliciana. She nodded to them and went to the bed to sit beside Tom.

'Well, as far as I can see, it's like this. Max – you saw a painting and you dreamt about that painting. Is that right?'

'Yes, but this is more than a dream, you know. I mean, I'm really here. Tom's really here.'

'So, somehow you have become part of the painting or the dream. Is that right?'

'Er ... yes. I suppose so.'

'Let's go back to the painting. What you saw on the painting was a girl in a tower and a dragon outside it. Is that right?' Max nodded.

'You automatically thought that the girl needed rescuing. In your dream, you bravely went about trying to do that. Am I right so far?' Max nodded again.

'Then Tom came to help you and here you both are. But you see, the girl in the tower does not need rescuing – I mean me of course. Nicholas, Dakas and Gemima are all my friends.' Aliciana stopped and looked at Max and Tom to see if they had anything to say.

After a few seconds, Max said 'You said I was brave, but I seem to have spent the whole time running away. I ran away from Dakas, I ran away from Nicholas, I nearly died of fright when I saw that spider and I even sat and cried in the forest. That doesn't sound very brave to me.' Max put his head down, afraid to look at any of them.

'Max, don't be so hard on yourself,' Aliciana said gently. 'You always intended on rescuing me, didn't you? You are here and if I needed to be rescued, you would do it, I know you would. But I am not the one that needs rescuing. That picture in the mirror you saw was Alicia. She is the one who needs you, not me. She has been brave all her life because she has had to be. Now is the time for her to look to you for help. I think it is time for this dream to end, don't you?' Max was about to answer when a familiar noise came from outside. They all went to look out of the window. Below, Dakas was flying around the castle, the trees swaying as his wings beat the air.

'I told you he was all right, didn't I?' said Nicholas with a big smile on his face. Max turned to reply but everything went black and he felt like he was floating on a cloud. He had never felt as relaxed as he felt at that moment. After a while, he drifted off to a dreamless sleep.

13

Company for Max

There had been great concern in West Hampstead for several days. It was thought that an unknown virus had swept through the two primary schools in the town. Fifty per cent of the children had been struck so badly by it that the schools were closed until the virus had died out. About twenty children had been admitted to hospital, Tom being one of them. There, the medical staff worked to keep the children's temperatures down. They found that after twenty-four hours of care, the children started to recover. Within a couple of days the virus started to go and by the time a week had passed, the illness was over. The doctors were quite baffled by it, saying that they had never seen anything like it before. Fortunately, all the children did recover and after three weeks, the schools were reopened.

Max's mum had worked very hard to reduce her son's fever. Dr Simmons had visited twice and by the evening, Max's temperature was more stable. He still remained in a deep sleep until two in the morning. His mum had stayed with him until 1.30 a.m. and then Dad had gone in to sit with him. Dad was wiping his son's brow with a cool cloth when Max suddenly opened his eyes. 'What happened to the dragon?' he asked in a croaky voice.

'Hush now, you've been dreaming Max. Go back to sleep. Everything is all right,' Dad replied, sounding very relieved.

'Everything's all right now,' muttered Max. Then he went back to sleep. Max woke in the morning coughing and sneezing. He was surprised that both his parents stayed at home that day. He had no idea how worried they had been. The virus had struck down another ten children on the same day as Max fell ill. It had been broadcast on the local TV channel and the whole town was talking about it.

Max slept a lot over the next couple of days. He didn't even try to think about his dream, for he felt too weak to concentrate on it all. He was also quite worried about Tom. His friend had been much worse than Max and it was a whole two days before the doctors were happy to say that he was at last making a recovery. They kept him in hospital for another day before his parents could take him home. Once Max was feeling better, he desperately wanted to see his friend, but his parents insisted he should wait until he was back to normal before he even stepped outside.

One of the things that Max wanted to talk to Tom about was the painting. As soon as he was well enough, Max looked beneath his bed. Somehow he knew that the painting would be gone. He felt as though the whole thing had just been a dream. It all seemed so unreal now. As time went by, Max really needed Tom to tell him that it was not just his imagination. He felt really frustrated because although he managed to speak to his friend on the phone, they were never alone. Then something happened that took all his attention away from the painting and the dreams.

'Max, there's something we want to talk to you about...' began Max's mum. She looked at her husband and he put a reassuring hand on hers.

'We've been quite concerned about you lately. We think maybe you need more company. I mean, more than your dad and me.'

'So you're going to let me go and see Tom then?' Max asked with a broad smile on his face.

'No, we're not talking about Tom, Max.'

'But I only want to see Tom. You know he's my best friend...'

'Yes – we know you want to see Tom and we'll take you over to see him soon,' interrupted Dad, 'but we're talking about someone else.'

'But I told you I only want to see Tom!' Max was feeling quite cross because he couldn't make out what his parents were trying to say.

'Now don't get cross, Max,' Mum said as she took his hands in hers. Max was drawn to her eyes and he knew that what she had to say was very important to her. 'You know some time back we were thinking of adopting a baby...' Max nodded. Max had a nasty feeling that they had found a baby and that this was their idea of company for him. He really didn't want to listen to any more, but he had no choice.

'Well, we knew you weren't very keen on that idea, so we've decided on something else,' Mum said quietly, all the while watching her son closely. 'We've decided to take in a little girl instead!' Mum could see that Max was not at all happy about this idea, but she continued hopefully. 'We thought perhaps a girl about your age?' Mum and Dad sat looking at their son. Max just sat opposite them staring straight ahead. There was an awkward silence in the room. Max's parents sat waiting for him to say something. Max was feeling cross, helpless and trapped.

Max remembered clearly the time when Mum had happily told him that they were going to adopt a baby. Max was only six and he was so angry. He could not understand why they should want another child. Surely, he thought, he was good enough for them? He didn't want to share his mum and dad with another child – especially not a baby. His cousin was only a few months old then and she cried all the time. Max could still see how his aunt and uncle had fussed around the baby and completely ignored their older son Ben. Ben was a right pain, too! He had torn Max's drawing of a horse that everyone said was really good. No, Max was glad that his parents had changed their minds about the whole thing.

Max sat looking at his parents. They looked very worried and he didn't like to see them like that. It would seem that they wanted his permission to take on another child. Part of Max wanted to scream and shout that he didn't want another person in their family ... but there was something telling him that he shouldn't. Suddenly, a picture of Aliciana came flooding into his mind. He remembered that she said he was brave. He also remembered that she said he should rescue Alicia. The memory of her crying came back clearly. He knew that it would be highly unlikely that they would adopt her, but he supposed that whoever the girl was, she would need rescuing just the same. To accept a stranger into the house would mean he would have to be very brave – he didn't know whether he was brave enough for that.

All these thoughts took only a few seconds to pass through Max's mind but to his parents, they seemed like a lifetime.

'I suppose,' said Max at last, 'I would be able to meet this girl.' Max could hardly believe what his mouth was saying. His head was telling him that he was making a big mistake and yet his heart was telling him to be brave.

'Yes, of course Max,' said his parents together. Max saw how relieved they looked. They smiled and hugged each other. Mum held Max tight and kissed his forehead. Dad said 'Another girl in the house; us boys will have to stick together, eh?' Dad winked and Max answered with a smile.

Then there was a lot of talk about meeting with the adoption society and taking time to get the right child. Max's parents assured him that they would not go ahead if he wasn't happy. Max sat back and watched his parents excitedly talking about the future.

That evening as Max settled down to sleep, he wondered whether he would ever dream about Aliciana, Dakas the Dragon, Gemima or Nicholas again. Not dreaming about that enormous spider would certainly be a good thing. He wondered whether the painting would reappear or whether he would ever work out what it all meant. He felt that he probably never would know. It had been a funny day. He had made a very important decision; a very brave one. He wondered if making important, brave decisions was a grown-up thing to do. Max didn't know, but he knew that it made him feel grown-up.

14

A New Member of the Family

In no time at all, life seemed to get back to normal. It wasn't long before Max was back at school. He and Tom then had plenty of time to talk over the strange events of the dreams. Tom had also had a dream on the night before they became ill, and he remembered it as just the same as Max's. It troubled him that he didn't know how he got from being under the great dragon to being in Aliciana's bedroom in the tower, although Max had told him that Nicholas had brought him up the stairs and placed him on the bed. Both boys went over and over their dreams but they couldn't work out what it all meant. The only thing that made any sense at all was that Max had agreed to consider having a girl to join his family. He felt sure in that way he would be rescuing a girl, although it would not be Alicia because she was much younger than him and his mum had clearly said that they would take someone the same age.

Days went by and turned into weeks. Gradually, both the boys started to forget all about the painting and the dreams. The only time they were reminded was when they bumped into Alicia in the playground, or when they saw the caretaker going about his work. Max knew that his parents were going through the process of getting another child, because of all the forms they were filling in and the interviews they were having with people who knew all about those things. Max sometimes wondered whether he really did want to 'rescue a girl' or whether he should just tell them that he'd changed his mind. Then he thought how excited his mum was getting and somehow he just couldn't find the words to say how he felt, so he tried hard not to think about it.

Then all of a sudden life got very busy. The end of term play was being rehearsed and Max, together with three other boys, was being a pirate. Tom was to be the ship's captain and both boys threw themselves into their parts with great enthusiasm. Mrs Pike felt that the sword fighting was in fact a little too enthusiastic. She spent a lot of time trying to calm the boys down, but often went home feeling that things were getting a little out of control. She wasn't sure if they would ever get a production that would be acceptable to show to the parents, let alone the school governors. She had thought about giving the boys different parts to play, something with less excitement in, but the boys had learnt their words really quickly and apart from the sword fighting, they were really good. So she struggled on in the hope that eventually it would all work out all right in the end. Max and Tom were totally unaware of their teacher's worries, because they were too busy having fun!

*   *   *

Some days before the dress rehearsal, Max's mum told him that they had arranged to meet a little girl. She said that they had looked at various other children, even a boy. They had settled on this particular girl because they felt she would settle well into the family in every way. Her name was Marie and she was six years old. Max said that he thought they would be getting someone the same age as him, but Mum explained that there were no girls of Max's age and they felt that this little girl really needed a home. Max thought about this for a while and was not at all sure that he wanted a little girl – who probably played with dollies – hanging around him. After all, he was nine and a half and she would be a real baby compared to him. Then his conversation with Aliciana came back to him. In his mind's eye he could almost see her frowning at him. So he said 'Okay' and rushed off to play on the computer.

The meeting was arranged for the next day at four o'clock. Max went home feeling very nervous. What if she were a cry-baby? What if she messed around with his stuff or wanted to have all the girly things on the television? What if she took all his parents' attention and they decided they didn't want him any more? What if she hated him? Or worse still, what if he hated her? It was all Max could do to keep control of his thoughts. Somehow he knew that this was what it meant to be brave, but deep down he didn't feel brave at all. He really wanted Tom to be with him but he knew that he had to do this on his own. Tom could not come and fight this dragon for him. This was his time to dig deep and find the courage that seemed so far away.

The day went much too quickly for Max; he was dreading the meeting. The afternoon had been particularly hard. Both he and Tom were excited that the whole afternoon would be given over to the play. Maybe, they thought later, they had been too excited. Mrs Pike had gone down with a heavy head cold and her patience was not as good as it normally was. The boys really enjoyed their roles and carried on the sword fighting for much longer than was necessary. Mrs Pike had got so angry that she had sent them to sit at the back of the hall, without their swords. The afternoon for Max was very boring and he couldn't help thinking about this girl that may soon become his sister. He wanted to talk to Tom about it but every time he opened his mouth, Mrs Pike was staring straight at him.

It seemed to Max as if time had speeded up that afternoon. He soon found himself in the back of the family car heading towards the meeting place. They arrived in good time at a block of offices on the edge of the town. Later, Max found he didn't remember walking from the car to the room where they were to meet Marie. As he looked up at a large clock on the wall of the room, he was sure that he would rather face Dakas again than be watching the hands move towards four o'clock. In fact, he felt sure anywhere would be better than there, in that pale blue room, with its comfy chairs and slightly battered coffee table.

Then the door opened and in came a tall lady holding a file. Max didn't notice much about her because he was looking at the figure that followed closely behind. For a moment, Max felt his heart miss a beat as he watched the girl standing shyly beside the lady. He was aware that people were speaking, but he didn't know what they were saying. Slowly, the girl raised her head and looked directly at Max.

'Alicia!' said Max in a voice of disbelief. Alicia smiled at Max. 'But... but Mum said the girl we were seeing was Marie!' Max glanced at his mum but she didn't offer an explanation.

'My name is really Marie, but I like to be called Alicia. It's my second name and it was my mother's name.'

'But Mum said you were only six. You look at least seven.' This made the adults laugh, but the children seemed not to notice.

'Well, I am six and three quarters,' replied Alicia as she stretched up to make herself look taller. This made the adults laugh some more but Max and Alicia continued not to hear it.

'So you are going to be my little sister! They were right. It was right. I'm totally flabbergasted!'

'I don't know what you're talking about Max but I do hope I'm going to be your sister. I do hope so, I really do.' Then Alicia threw herself at Max. She clung on to him as though she would never let him go. Max felt very uncomfortable at this display of affection and he squirmed. 'This,' he thought, 'is where I have to be brave.'

Max could not wait to tell Tom about his new 'sister'. Tom was amazed how it had turned out.

'So,' he said, 'the painting, the dreams, they were all pointing to Alicia becoming your sister then?'

'Looks like it. How bizarre!'

'It was a really exciting adventure and seemed so real! I wonder what's happened to the painting? Do you think it's made its way up to your loft again?'

'I don't know, but I'm going to get up there and look as soon as I get the chance, I can tell you!'

'There's so much we don't know though, isn't there?'

'Well, I've solved some of the mystery,' Max said, watching Tom's eager face.

'What's that then? Come on ... tell me. I know you're bursting to!'

'When I had chance to tell Alicia all about it she went very quiet. Then she pulled out her favourite books from her bag. You'll never guess!'

'Oh Max ... come on, tell me or there'll be trouble!' said Tom, excitedly.

'One is *Alice in Wonderland* and there's a picture of the rabbit just as we saw it, pocket watch and all. Alicia said it was her favourite part of the book. Then she had a nursery rhyme book and there was one in there called "Little Miss Muffet"!' Max looked at Tom's face, but his friend showed no sign that he knew what Max was talking about.

'Little Miss Muffet and her spider? Miss Gemima Muffet?' prompted Max.

'Miss Gemima Muffet! You mean the girl with the pet spider?'

'The same one; even the cream dress and blonde

hair! I must say the spider didn't look half as big in the book. Then she had another book about a castle and a dragon. Can you believe it?'

'It's just amazing, incredible and any other big word that I can't think of at the moment! Hey, what about the man with the beard, or should I say, the caretaker?'

'Now, this is something you won't believe. Alicia's other book is one about Father Christmas!'

'Father Christmas?'

'Yes, Father Christmas – or should I say Saint Nicholas?'

'Wow! That is unbelievable.' The boys stood looking at each other, letting it all sink in.

'That would be why he is a caretaker then,' said Tom at last.

'Why?'

'It's a job that gives him time off at Christmas.'

'You mean ... he really is Father Christmas?'

'Well Max,' smiled Tom, 'I wouldn't be surprised, would you?'

'After all that's happened over the last few months, no, I wouldn't be at all surprised! I'll tell you what though; I've missed the painting and the dreams. It was a real adventure, wasn't it?'

'It certainly was. But you never know, that painting may still be in your loft somewhere. Maybe there's another adventure to have!'

Max sighed as he climbed into bed that night and thought about all that had happened. A shaft of light came through the gap in the curtains and Max watched it shimmering into the room; he could see gold and silver stars bouncing about in the light. Max turned over and closed his eyes. He had a smile on his face because he could smell the wonderful fragrance of roses, vanilla ice cream and strawberries.